words by **MICHAEL DAHL**

pictures by **OMAR LOZANO**

Sweet Dreams,
SUPERGIRL™

Supergirl based on characters created by
JERRY SIEGEL and **JOE SHUSTER**
by special arrangement with the Jerry Siegel family

PICTURE WINDOW BOOKS
a Capstone imprint

From sun-soaked morning . . .

. . . until moonlit night . . .

A hero bursts with POW!-WHAM!-BOOM! energy . . .

Each day, a hero is ready for another adventure . . .

. . . and each night, she'll have a story to share.

Each day, a hero welcomes helping hands . . .

All day, a super hero travels far and wide . . .

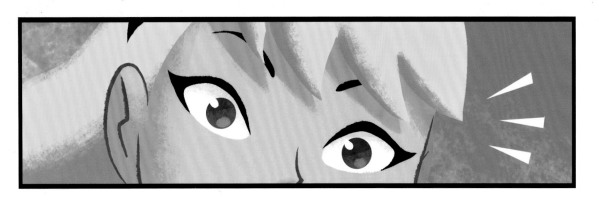

All day, a hero faces many challenges alone.

But at night,
others are
always there
for her.

For a hero, the day is breathless, nonstop action . . .

. . . so night is time to relax, breathe easy.

A super hero bravely faces each and every day.

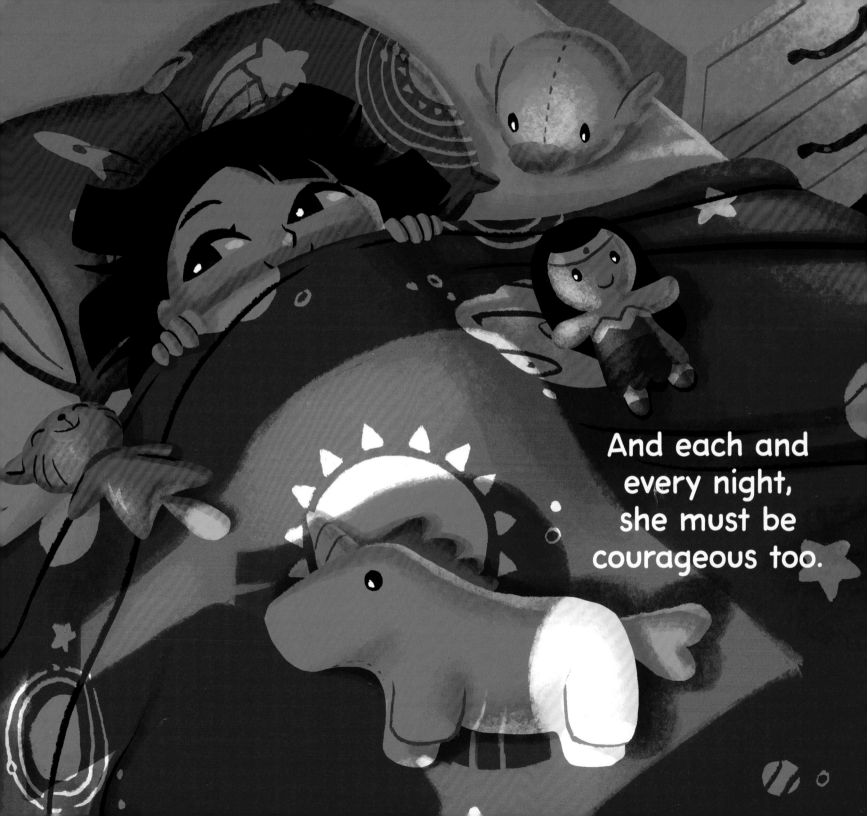

And each and every night, she must be courageous too.

During the day, a hero may feel weak at times . . .

. . . so at night, she will recharge.

. . . the time has come to rest them.

Tomorrow, once again . . .

. . . the world
needs a hero . . .

. . . to soar . . .

Sweet dreams, Supergirl.

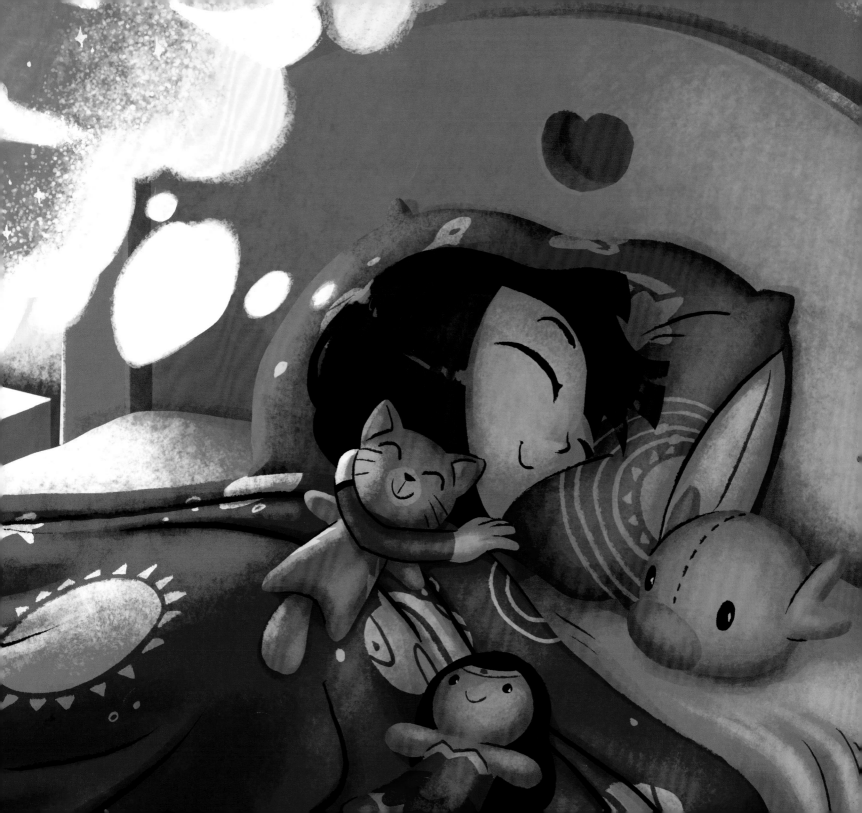

Sweet Dreams CHECKLIST!

☐
Share Stories

☐ Say Goodnight

☐ Snuggle Up

☐ Breathe Easy

☐ Stay Brave

☐
Dream Big